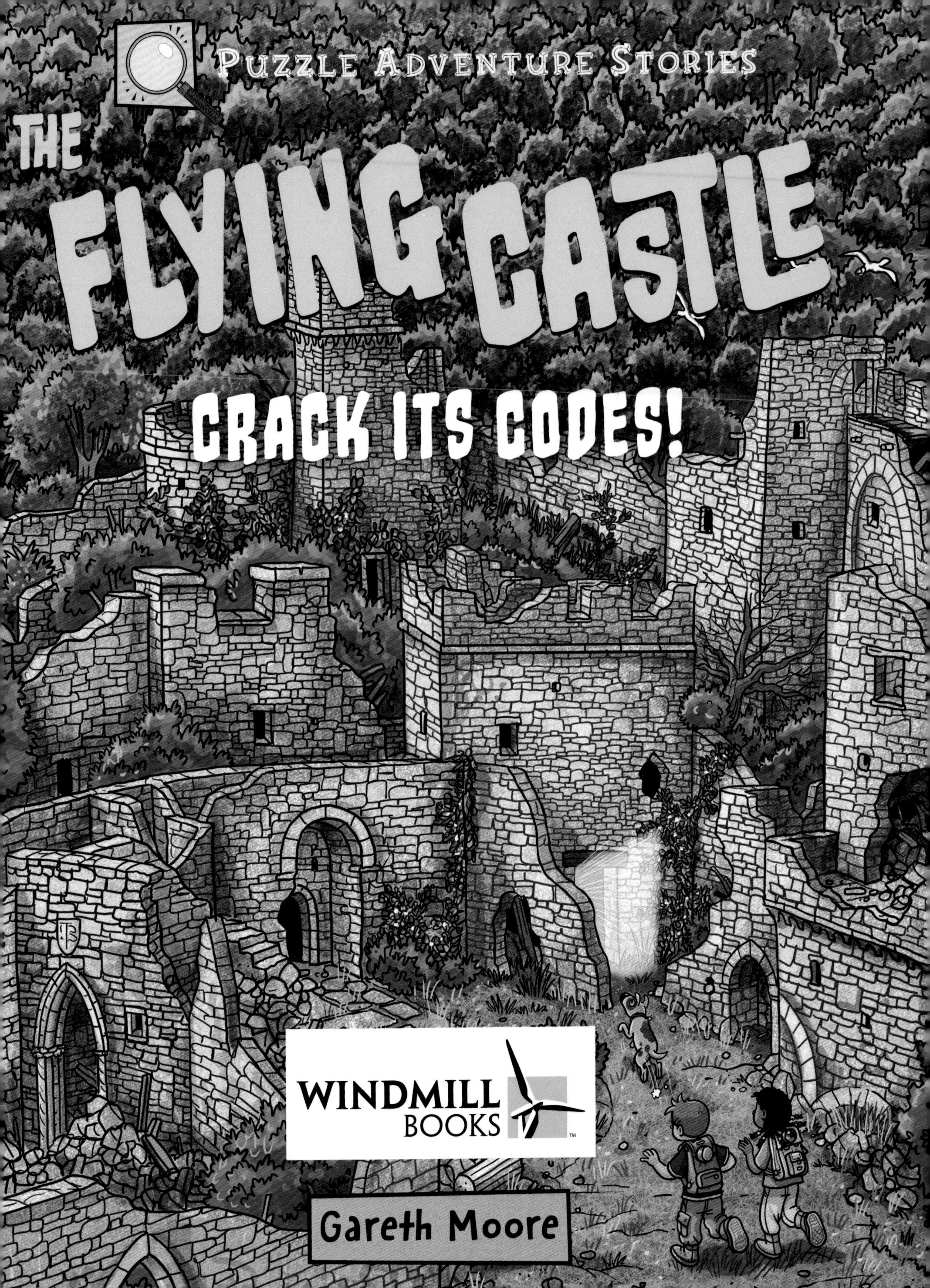
PUZZLE ADVENTURE STORIES
THE FLYING CASTLE
CRACK ITS CODES!
WINDMILL BOOKS
Gareth Moore

Published in 2019 by **Windmill Books**, an imprint of Rosen Publishing
29 East 21st Street, New York, NY 10010

Written by Gareth Moore
Illustrated by Moreno Chiacchiera
Designed by Paul Oakley, with Emma Randall
Edited by Frances Evans, with Julia Adams

Cataloging-in-Publication Data

Names: Moore, Gareth.
Title: The flying castle / Gareth Moore.
Description: New York : Windmill Books, 2019. | Series: Puzzle adventure stories
Identifiers: LCCN ISBN 9781508195382 (pbk.) | ISBN 9781508196273 (library bound) | ISBN 9781508195399 (6 pack)
Subjects: LCSH: Castles--Juvenile fiction. | Puzzles--Juvenile fiction.
Classification: LCC PZ7.M5565 Fl 2019 | DDC [E]--dc23

Manufactured in the United States of America

CPSIA Compliance Information: Batch #BS18WM: For Further Information contact Rosen Publishing, New York, New York at 1-800-237-9932

Let's Get Started!

Ruby, her best friend Ned, and her dog, Mungo, are visiting the ruins of an ancient castle. Mungo, who is leading the way, runs ahead. Will you join the three of them as they explore the castle and help discover its surprising secrets? Have a pen and some paper at the ready to help them solve any puzzles along the way! You can find the answers starting on page 29.

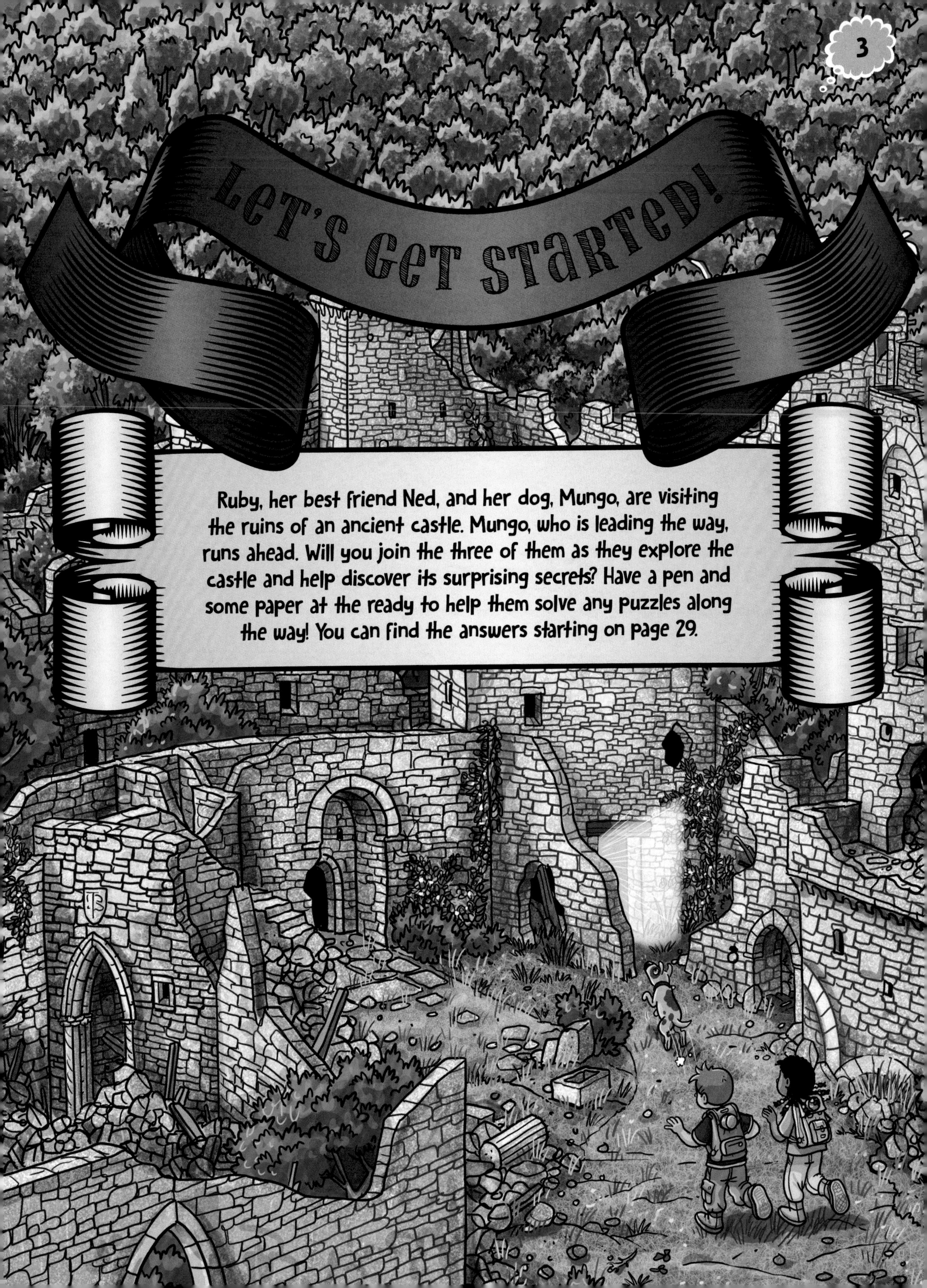

The Mysterious Panel
Ruby and Ned enter the castle, and step into a room that looks as if it was used by knights hundreds of years ago. The children are about to leave when they realize Mungo is not with them. Where can he have gone?
There is a secret door hidden in the fireplace.
Mungo?

Roundabout Writing

Ruby pulls at the boards over the fireplace and they come loose. Hidden behind is a concealed corridor, leading to a room with a strange machine in the middle. This machine doesn't look medieval! What can it be for? Ruby hopes it is not dangerous, as Mungo seems to have climbed inside it and become stuck. Perhaps finding the missing cogs will free Mungo. Can you figure out where they are?

Spied a Spider?

Ruby and Ned spot the trapdoor that hides the missing cogs. They want to open it, but there is a bug on top. Is it safe to open? Neds knows that the black creeper spider is very dangerous, but the similar-looking black creeper insect is harmless. Which is it?

Under the Floor

Aha! The missing cogs! Ruby finds a note, too. She reads it out loud. "To ★ make + the ★ machine + work, ★ you + need ★ only + two ★ cogs." But which ones? Can you find them?

Buttoned Up

Ned fits the cogs to the machine, and they start to turn. A panel slides back to reveal a keyboard. A mechanical voice says "Type the password!" Ned looks confused ... but Ruby has an idea! What does she do?

8
Falling Rocks
As Ned pulls the handle, the glass cover vanishes, freeing Mungo. However, a moment later, the room shudders. Large chunks of stone drop from the ceiling.
3
7
15
11
31
5
29
13
37
19
The mechanical voice speaks again, with a crackle. "Which number doesn't belong?" Ned shouts out the answer. What is it?

Flee the Room

After Ned shouts, the rocks stop falling. The doorway has been partly blocked, but there is a small gap for the kids to squeeze through. A countdown begins! Can you use your finger to trace the fastest route to leave the room?

Each arrow shows how many seconds it takes to travel that way.

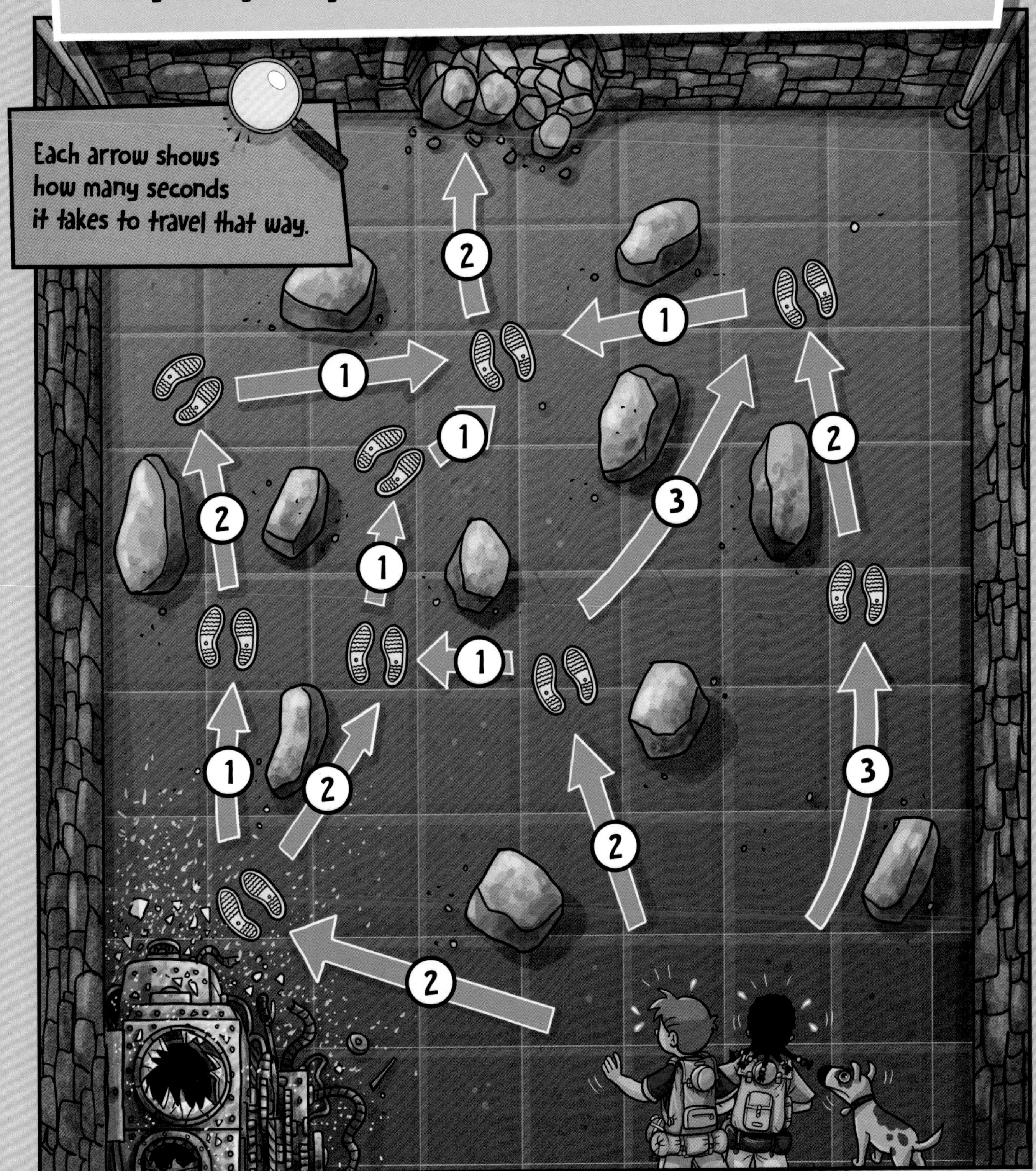

a Better View
They follow the passageway into a new room, where a clear blue sky is visible. Where are they? Ruby decides to climb up to the window to take a look. Can you help her reassemble the ladder by placing the pieces in the correct order?
CLUE:
Look at the ends of the ladder pieces to see how they fit together.
A
B
C
D

The Magic Castle

Ruby looks out of the window and is astonished by what she sees. They are very high up, and the view is slowly moving. "The castle is flying!" Luckily, Ruby spots something that may give them a clue as to what is going on. Can you find it, too?

Coded Message

Tucked beneath the windowsill, Ruby finds a folded piece of paper. They open it and discover a secret code! Some of the letters have been translated into English, but not all of them. Can you figure out what the missing words say by comparing the matching symbols? Write the message down on your piece of paper.

The Knights' Watch

The message seems useless, but Ruby puts the paper in her pocket anyway. Ruby, Ned, and Mungo continue through the castle. In the next room are some mechanical knights, holding fearsome-looking weapons. The children decide it is best to avoid them! Can you find a safe route through the room, without making them start moving? Trace the safe pathway with your finger.

The Room of Fires

They manage to sneak past the knights without being seen, and make it safely into the next room. It's wonderfully warm, but it's not clear where they should go next. Perhaps there is another exit hidden in a fireplace? Have they already found a clue that could help them?

28
3
15
7
12
38
24

What did that secret code say, Ruby?

There is only one bucket of water, so they should choose wisely which fire to extinguish to reveal a secret exit.

Inside the Castle Walls

Ned, Ruby, and Mungo crawl carefully through the fireplace. The floor is still a little hot! They find themselves in a narrow corridor, which they soon discover is part of a maze of secret passages hidden within the castle walls! Can you help them find their way to the door? Trace the path with your finger.

The children can go up and down the ladders, and jump over the gaps in the floor. However, once they drop through a trapdoor, they can't go back!

Skeleton Key

Made it! Ruby, Ned, and Mungo emerge from the maze of passages into a dusty room, which was probably once the castle dungeon. Ned soon finds out that the door out of this room is locked. One of the skeletons is holding the correct key, but can you figure out which one?

a Medieval Feast
They unlock the door and step through into what appears to be a medieval hall. A feast is in full swing! A serving boy approaches them. "Please can you help us find our way out of this castle?" says Ned. "Of course," says the serving boy, whose name is Jack. "But first, you must solve my riddle!"
Riddle me this. Who is in charge of this castle? They have a woman to their left, blue eyes, and they are right-handed.
Food!

The Kitchen Door

Jack tells them to meet him in the kitchen. Which of these doors should they go through? There might be a clue if you remember what he was wearing.

The Kitchen

Jack has to finish his tasks before he can show the children which way to go. Can you help him?

I need to serve a food made from these ingredients.

flour
yeast
salt

The Missing Silverware

Poor Jack! He was just about to take Ned and Ruby to the secret passageway, but he has been given two more urgent jobs to do first. Ned and Ruby do their best to help him. The first task is to find some silverware.

Juicy bones!

Can you help me find knives, forks, and spoons? I need two of each!

Quick on the Drawer

The Secret Panel

At last, Jack's tasks are complete! Now he can finally help Ruby, Ned, and Mungo find their way out of the castle. Jack tells them that one of the paintings on this wall is a secret panel. It will open if tapped in the right way—but where is it hidden?

The Knight's Door
The secret panel swings open and the children step in. Jack tells them they need to go through the "right knight's door" to continue. There are four doors in this corridor, but which one did Jack mean?
What would the "right knight's door" look like?
Maybe it has something to do with the knights we saw earlier?

The Knights' Revenge

The door opens into a large room where mechanical knights are standing guard. "Not again!" groans Ned. The serving boy, Jack, has to get back to his chores. Before he goes, he says, "Only step on the six-sided stones." Can you find a route to the other side, without waking the knights? Trace it with your finger.

The Control Room

Well now, this is not something you expect in a medieval castle! However, this is a rather strange castle, after all. This control panel will help Ruby and Ned get back home, if only they can figure out how it works.

Using the controls in this room, you can command the castle to fly wherever you wish. But first, you must enter the right code.

Look carefully across each row and down each column. Then decide the order to press each button on the panel below!

Returning Home

Before they can return the castle to where it came from, Ned and Ruby need to figure out where they found it! There are several clearings where the castle could land. Figure out where they should guide it to.

Park the Castle

Ruby and Ned program the destination into the computer. A screen lights up on the control panel, as the castle makes its final calculations for returning home. Each line contains a number sequence, but each one is missing a vital number. Can you figure out the correct values to enter into the computer?

Leaving the Castle

The castle has landed safely, and is back to its old, ruined appearance. Ruby, Ned, and Mungo need to get back down to the ground. The computer says, "Only use the ladders with an odd number of rungs." How do they do it? Trace the path they use with your finger.

Down from the Walls

They are almost at the bottom, but wait! Not everything has gone back to normal. There are still some mechanical knights around. Some are even camouflaged! How many are there? If Ned and Ruby can find them all, they can creep past!

Goodbye!

Ruby, Ned, and Mungo creep past all of the knights and make it safely out of the castle. When they are a safe distance away, they turn around to look. The ruins are exactly as they found them at the start of their adventure, and all traces of the medieval occupants are now gone—or are they? Can you spot what Ruby and Ned have seen?

Answers

Page 4 The backward writing on the scroll reads: "There is a secret door hidden in the fireplace.."

Page 5 The letters on the machine spell the word TRAPDOOR.

Page 6 (top) The bug is an insect, as it has six legs and not eight. The children are safe to lift the trapdoor.

Page 6 (bottom)

Page 7 Ruby types "the password," looking at the small letters on the keypad. "8, 4, 3, 7, 2, 7, 7, 9, 6, 7, 3."

Page 8 All the numbers on the rocks are prime numbers, except for 15, which is a multiple of 3 and 5.

Page 9 The fastest route takes 7 seconds.

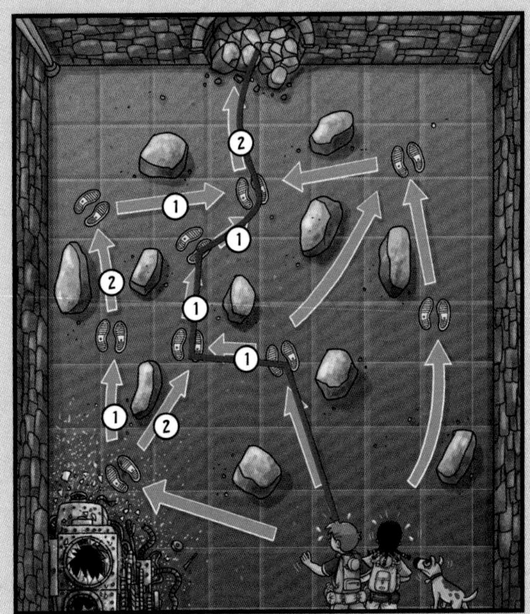

Page 10 Ruby pieces together the ladder from top to bottom in this order: C, D, A, B.

Page 11

Page 12 The message reads: "When fighting fire choose a multiple of both three and eight."

Page 13

Page 14 They should choose the fireplace marked 24, as that is a multiple of 3 and 8.

Page 15

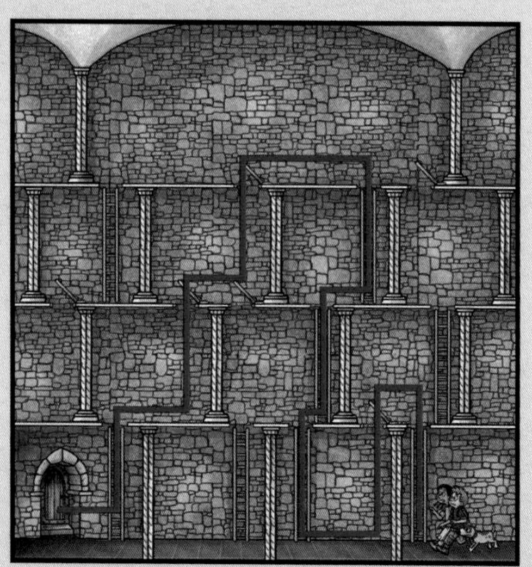

Page 16

Page 17

Page 18 (top)

Page 18 (bottom) Jack needs to serve bread.

Page 19 (top)

Page 19 (bottom) The items should be placed in the drawer in this order: knives, spoons, forks.

Page 20 The secret passageway is behind this picture.

Page 21 The knight's shield matches the shields of the knights on page 13.

Page 22

Page 23 There should be one of each symbol in each row and column. Press the buttons in this order:
1 = bird 2 = arrow
3 = star 4 = sword

Page 24 The children walked this way, and the castle was in the top right clearing.

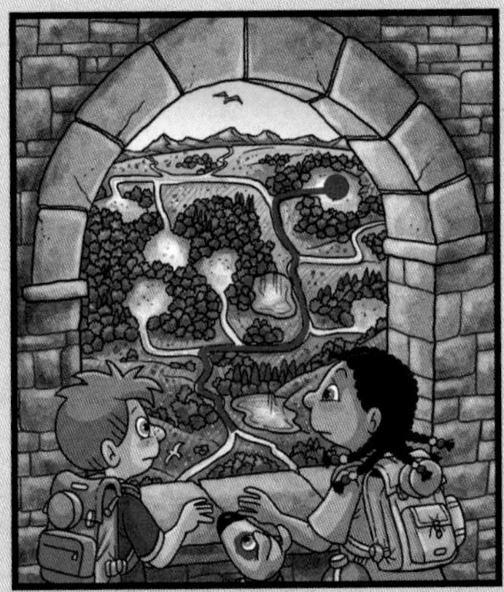

Page 25 4 7 10 13 16 – each number is 3 more than the one before.
27 22 17 12 7 – each number is 5 less than the one before.
2 4 8 16 32 – each number is double the one before.
45 41 37 33 29 – each number is 4 less than the one before.

Page 26

Page 27 There are nine knights hidden in the picture.

Page 28 Ruby and Ned can see Jack, the serving boy they met.

Glossary

chores Tasks, often to do with the household.

dungeon An underground prison cell in a castle.

extinguish To put out (a fire).

medieval To do with the Middle Ages.

occupant A person who is in a building or car.

rung A step on a ladder.

Further Information

Books:

Kamigaki, Hiro. *Pierre the Maze Detective: The Search for the Stolen Maze Stone.* London, UK: Lawrence King, 2015.

Smith, Sam. *Map Maze Book.* London, UK: Usborne Publishing, 2017.

Tallarico, Tony J. *Spot-the-Differences Around the World.* London, UK: Dover Children's, 2009.

Websites

For web resources related
to the subject of this book, go to:
www.windmillbooks.com/weblinks
and select this book's title.

Index